CREPE-ING CONCERNS

CROOKED BAY COZY MYSTERIES, BOOK 6

PATTI BENNING

SUMMER PRESCOTT BOOKS PUBLISHING

CHAPTER ONE

Theresa Tremblay hummed a little as she flipped the sign on the Crooked Crêperie's door from open to closed. It was a sunny summer day, and she had the rest of the afternoon and evening to enjoy the benefits of living in a town on a bay right off of Lake Huron. She was looking forward to a walk along the beach after she closed the restaurant.

Kian, one of two employees that she had hired so far, was already wiping down the tables. After that, she knew he would sweep and mop the floor, empty the garbage, and bring in the day's mail before clocking out. The entire process would take him another ten or fifteen minutes. It was a rare day that Theresa or any of her employees stayed at work past three thirty. The trade-off was that her day started before seven every morning, but she thought it was worth it. There was nothing quite like having every evening free to convince her moving to Crooked Bay and opening a restaurant had been the right choice.

While Kian cleaned, she whipped up the batter for one last crêpe. It wasn't for a customer, but rather for her own late lunch. After she spooned the batter onto the griddle, she opened the small fridge behind the counter and considered their ingredients. She didn't have a particular menu item in mind, so she figured she might as well use up the rest of the fresh ingredients they had left over from the day, since they would just be discarded otherwise.

"Green onions, peppers, tomatoes … hmm. I'll use the rest of this ham too."

"Sounds like it might make a decent omelet," Kian said as he walked by with the broom.

An omelet did sound good, actually, but she didn't feel like cracking open an egg, scrambling it, and having to clean up all the dishes she used to do so before she left. She settled on a bit of shredded cheddar cheese instead and laid out the toppings generously once the crêpe was ready to receive them.

She had her food packed up in a to-go container by the time Kian came over to the computer and clocked out. He left a moment later, and as the crêperie's door shut behind him, Theresa sat back on her stool and closed her eyes, basking in the silence for a second. She liked both of her employees, she really did, but there is something special about being alone in her restaurant after hours like this. It reminded her of those first two months when she had run the place on her own. It had been a busy time, and wasn't something she wanted to repeat, but it had been immensely satisfying as well. The crêperie had become like a second home to her. Or maybe a first home—she felt more attached to this place than she did to her apartment.

She took her time wiping off the griddle, cleaning up the kitchen, and tidying up the rest of the restaurant. It was barely past three thirty by the time she stepped out of the employee entrance at the back of the building and got into her car.

She drove through town with the windows down. It was hot out, but being so close to one of the Great Lakes meant there was usually at least something of a breeze, and the fresh air beat her car's air conditioning any day. The beachside park just out of town on her way home was crowded, so she passed it by, turned north, and followed the road along the lake's coast up to her apartment building. It was a small building, with only eight units, and was far enough out of town that it was surrounded by nothing but grass, trees, and across the road from it, the shining waves of Lake Huron.

She hit her blinker, slowed her car, and turned into the parking lot. She knew her neighbors' cars by sight, so the one vehicle that didn't belong there caught her attention right away. It was a tan sedan, nothing that would have caught her eye in other circumstances. She dismissed it at first, figuring someone else in the building had a guest over, but as she pulled past the vehicle into her customary parking spot near the building's front door, her eyes landed on the man who was sitting in the driver's seat.

If he had been on his phone or eating food or even reading a book, he might not have caught her attention, but he was just sitting there, staring at the building like he was waiting for something to happen. It made the hair on the back of her neck stand up.

He's probably just waiting for someone, she told herself, but it didn't make the unsettled feeling in the pit of her stomach go away. He was parked in the back row of spots, facing the building. She could see him if she looked in her rearview mirror. She reached for her door handle, but hesitated. She wasn't sure whether she should just go in or ask him what he was doing. If he was up to no good, simply knowing someone had seen his face might be enough to discourage him.

Maybe she was just being paranoid.

She hesitated and glanced in the rearview mirror again. She could have sworn his eyes met hers, but it was impossible to tell for sure. In the next second, she saw him reach down, start his engine, and buckle his seatbelt. He drove forward and turned out of the lot, speeding off down the road toward town.

A little shaken, Theresa grabbed her purse and her to-go box and got out of her car. None of the other vehicles in the lot were out of place, but she felt wary as she walked up to the apartment building's door and let herself inside.

She felt a little better when she was in her own apartment with the door locked behind her. She had been planning to eat her crêpe out on the patio while enjoying her view of the bay, but she wasn't so sure she wanted to anymore.

As much as she tried to convince herself that she was making a big deal out of nothing, she couldn't get the intense way the man had been watching the apartment building out of her mind, or how he had left right after their eyes met in her rearview mirror. She wished she'd thought to take a picture of him or his vehicle with her phone, but it was too late for that now. She would just have to be prepared if she saw him again—and she'd make extra sure her windows and doors were locked, on the off chance he was casing the building for a way in.

Instead of her nice, late lunch out on her patio enjoying the summer afternoon, she sat at the dining room table inside her apartment. The food was still good, of course, and her apartment was tidy and comfortable, but her meal felt a little sad, sitting indoors alone like this. She missed her late husband, Nicolas. She missed Jace, her son, who had moved to the Upper Peninsula a couple of months ago. She even missed her neighbor's dog, Atticus. She had watched him for a week and a half the month before, and had gotten used to having him around to keep her company.

She was lonely.

Oh, not all the time. She chatted with her employees at work and knew a lot of her regulars by name. She had acquaintances and even friends in town that she saw on a regular basis. She either called or saw her cousin, Clare, almost daily, and she had gone on a few casual dates with the man who owned the local used bookstore.

But before this, for most of her adult life, she lived

with her family. She'd had her husband and her son around almost constantly, and for a portion of those years, she'd had a beloved dog as well. She didn't think she had ever in her life spent this much time alone. Before she married Nicolas, she'd been in college and had a roommate, and before that she lived with her parents. She kept thinking she would get used to it, to coming home to an empty apartment and having no one to talk to in the evenings. It wasn't like she hated it. It was very freeing to be able to come home and just do whatever she wanted, whether that meant watching television, deep cleaning the kitchen, or going back out for dinner or just a walk along the beach.

But sometimes, when she least expected it, her solitary life would start to bring her down. She sighed, took another bite of her crêpe—which really would have been better with some scrambled eggs inside it—and stared out the patio window. The day was so gorgeous. She had no right to feel as morose as she did, so she tried to cheer herself up by planning out her week. She had Wednesday off, and she wanted to experiment with some new recipes that day. Clare was supposed to come over to be her guinea pig, and they had a double date planned for that evening.

That was only two days away. Tomorrow, she would—

A knock at her door interrupted her thoughts. She got up, walking away from her lonely meal, and peeked out the peephole. Her neighbor, Grace, and a woman she didn't recognize were standing outside her door. She turned the deadbolt and pulled the door open, only to be body-slammed by a large, grey-blue dog with a blocky head.

"Hey, you handsome guy," she said as she crouched to scratch behind the dog's ears and pat his rib cage. "I miss having you around." She straightened up after a moment. "Hi, Grace. I don't think I've met your friend."

Normally, her enthusiastic greeting of the dog combined with a simple hello to his owner made Grace laugh, but now that she had gotten a good look at her, she realized her friend looked drawn and worried. "Can we come in?"

"Of course," Theresa said, stepping out of the doorway. The two women and the dog came through the door, and Grace shut and locked it behind her. Theresa felt the back of her neck prickle again. "Is something wrong?"

The other woman took a deep breath. "I think someone is stalking me. I think I might be in danger."

CHAPTER TWO

Theresa's mind immediately flashed to the man she'd seen in the parking. She gestured to her couch. "Sit down, both of you. You can let Atticus go."

Grace unclipped the dog's leash, and Atticus started sniffing around at all the new smells that had gotten into her apartment since he was last there.

"First, I should introduce you to my friend, Molly," she said. "Molly, this is Theresa, the neighbor I was telling you about. She's the one who watched Atticus for me."

"It's nice to meet you," Molly said. She looked to be about Grace's age, so a few years younger than Theresa. She had pale, strawberry-blonde hair and a kind smile, which she directed at Theresa.

"It's nice to meet you too," Theresa said, shaking her hand.

"Molly agreed to come stay with me for a few days, but I wanted to let you know what's going on too, both because you're my neighbor and it might affect you, and because I was hoping you might have some advice."

Theresa sat on the armchair, kitty-corner from the two women on the couch. Atticus came over and rested his big head on her lap, and she stroked his fur idly. "Tell me what's going on."

Grace took a deep breath. "It's … complicated. I don't want to get into all of the details, but after my mom's death—" She broke off to squeeze her eyes shut. Theresa felt her heart clench. Grace had flown out to spend time with her mother during her last days, and she knew losing her had been hard on the other woman. "After my mom's death and I came back here, I've had one creepy experience after the other. I saw someone looking in my patio window late one night, and I swear I've seen the same person watching me in town too. And someone tried to open my apartment door the other night. This morning, someone called me from an unknown number, and when I answered, all I heard was breathing. I feel like I'm going crazy."

"The person you saw looking through your window, did he have dark hair?" Theresa asked.

Grace's eyes widened. "He did. How did you know?"

"There was a stranger in the parking lot when I pulled in. He was parked so he could watch the building, and he was just sitting in his car, staring at the door. Once he saw me looking at him, he left. He had dark hair, but that's the only feature I could really identify."

"That was today?" Grace asked, shooting a glance toward Theresa's patio door, which looked out at the corner of the parking lot.

"Yes. Not even twenty minutes ago. Do you have any idea who he is?"

"I don't," Grace said. "I only saw him well enough through the window to get a vague impression of him. Dark-haired, tall … if I'm being honest, I thought it might have been my ex-boyfriend at first, but when I called to confront him about it, he acted clueless."

"Have you gone to the police?" Theresa asked.

Grace hesitated, shook her head. "I… I know I should, but I'm just going to sound crazy. The only thing that has actually happened was the guy looking in my window the one time. And he wasn't standing right against the glass or anything. He was a little way away, in the grass. He could have easily just been walking by behind the apartment building. As soon as I spotted him, he hurried on his way. I'll just sound crazy if I tell them everything. I don't want to involve them unless I have to. I'm hoping it will blow over soon." She exchanged a glance with Molly. Theresa got the feeling there was something they weren't sharing with her.

"I'll keep an eye out and let you know if I see that man again, or anyone else who seems suspicious. Is there anything else I can do?"

"I don't think so. I mostly just wanted to give you a heads-up. You might want to be a little more careful about locking your doors, keep your eyes peeled if you get home after dark, that sort of thing. I've been debating telling you or not because I didn't want to worry you if I'm just imagining things, but I'd feel horrible if I didn't tell you and something happened."

"I appreciate it," Theresa said. "And I believe you. Don't hesitate to call me or come over if you need anything, Grace. That goes for either of you—you're welcome to come to me for help too, Molly."

"Thanks," she said. "I'm not sure how long I'll be staying. I work remotely too, though for a different company than Grace is with. We should both be here for most of the day, but knowing I can pop right next door if I'm alone and something happens makes me feel better."

"Us women have to stick together," Theresa said. She turned to look out her patio window, wishing her gut hadn't been right about that man she'd seen in the parking lot. The surge of loneliness from earlier was gone, but she wished it would come back. It was a lot better than this. Being worried about a friend was never a good feeling.

She didn't blame her friend in the slightest, but her conversation with Grace and Molly destroyed any hope she had of enjoying the lovely summer evening. Instead of going out for a walk or finding a trail to hike after they left, she stayed inside and did some research on her laptop about stalking, stalkers, and the crime statistics surrounding the subject.

Nothing she was reading made her feel any better, so before it got dark, she pulled her blinds shut and tried to find a good movie on the television to distract herself with. She always felt a little guilty about time wasted in front of the TV. It was hard to convince herself that it wasn't wasted time, that there wasn't something else she should be doing.

It was astounding how free her life was now that

she didn't work overtime and the only one she was taking care of was herself.

She checked the apartment building's parking lot when she left for work the next morning and was relieved to see that the only cars there were the ones that belonged there. Grace must have picked Molly up when she came to stay. She was glad Grace had someone with her, because she found herself worrying about them on and off during her hours at the crêperie.

Wynne, her other employee, noticed and commented on it. "Is everything all right? You seem distracted."

She said that when Theresa almost put onions on a banana and hazelnut spread crêpe, the second time she had almost messed up an order that day. "I just have some personal stuff going on," Theresa said. She didn't think Grace would want her to share the details of what was happening. "It's nothing major, but it's been on my mind since last night."

"Do you want me to take over at the griddle?"

Theresa laughed. "Yeah, that might be a smart idea. I'll handle the food prep and taking orders for a while. Thanks, Wynne."

She did her best to focus on work after that. It wasn't fair of her to make things harder for Wynne just because she was distracted. She might be the boss, but as far as she was concerned that meant it was her responsibility to lead by example, not to force others to make up for her shortcomings.

She managed to focus on work for a while until a woman who looked enough like Grace that it made her do a double take came into the crêperie and approached the counter. She had the same dark hair but was a little taller and a little younger looking. Theresa could tell when she spoke that she wasn't from around here—her voice had a faint southern accent that marked her as from out of state right away.

"Oh, man, it's been forever since I've had a good crêpe," the woman said. "Can I have your special?"

This week's special was a sweet crêpe with a blackberry reduction and freshly made crème fraiche, topped with powdered sugar. It was popular enough she was thinking of adding it to the menu permanently.

"Of course," Theresa said, smiling. "Will that be for here or to go?"

"For here, I guess," the woman said, glancing around. "You take cards, right?"

Theresa nodded. She accepted the woman's credit card and ran it, then handed it back to her. The woman moved over to watch Wynne make her crêpe while Theresa took the next order. There was no one else waiting in line, so she started wiping down the tables until the first order was up. She carried the crêpe over to the woman, who had taken a table by the window. She was on the phone when Theresa approached, and she overheard the last part of their conversation.

"Thanks. I miss you too. I haven't spoken to Grace yet, but I'll tell you when I do." She paused. "Yeah. I'm hoping I'll be back soon. I've got to go—my food's here."

She hung up and looked at Theresa for a second before Theresa realized she was staring and it was probably making her customer uncomfortable. She put the plate down on the table and said, "Enjoy! Don't hesitate to let us know if you need anything else." She gave her best customer service smile, then turned and hurried back to the counter before the expression could fade.

She wouldn't have thought anything of it the day before, but now she couldn't help but fixate on the name she'd overheard. Had this woman been talking about Grace, her neighbor? It was a common name—it almost had to be a coincidence, didn't it?

She watched the woman as she ate her crêpe, but

she didn't take her phone out again, and she didn't do anything that raised any red flags. Finally, when she noticed that Wynne kept giving her concerned looks, she forced herself to look away.

She was being paranoid. That was all there was to it.

CHAPTER THREE

There was no stranger parked in front of the apartment building when Theresa returned home that afternoon, but there *was* a woman with a dog waiting for her. She felt a surge of concern when she saw Grace standing outside the door with Atticus, but her friend greeted her with a smile and a small wave.

Theresa got out of her car. "Everything alright?"

"Yeah, nothing weird has happened since yesterday. I was just wondering if you wanted to take a walk. Molly has a video call for work, and Atticus was being loud, so I decided to take him out. Then I realized you'd be back soon, so I figured it wouldn't hurt to wait and see if you were interested in joining us."

"Sure," Theresa said. She bent to greet Atticus, who was as excited to see her as ever, and then straightened up. "Just down the beach?"

Grace nodded, and the three of them set out across the road. The narrow, sandy path down to the beach was familiar enough by now that Theresa could probably have walked it with her eyes closed. It was the main reason she'd chosen her particular apartment, and she enjoyed living right on Crooked Bay just as much as she thought she would.

Now that summer was in full swing, even this usually quiet strip of the beach had a handful of other visitors on it, so Grace kept Atticus on his leash as they walked. The dog tugged at the end of it, shoving his nose into the sand and snorting with such force that Theresa wondered how he didn't inhale the sand into his lungs. He seemed unbothered, not even coughing before he found the next spot that warranted a good sniff.

"Thanks again for watching him," Grace said. "I know I've said it a lot, but I still feel bad for leaving him with you at the last minute, and for so long too."

"Like I already said, I really didn't mind," Theresa said. "I enjoyed having him around. Liam did too—he keeps asking me if I'm going to bring Atticus around to the bookstore again."

Grace smiled. "You're free to borrow him for an evening whenever you want. Are you and Liam still dating?"

"Casually," Theresa said. She didn't know why she felt like she needed to clarify that to everyone who asked, but she did.

"How many dates is this now?" Grace asked, a teasing note in her voice. "Are either of you seeing anyone else?"

"I don't know if he is," Theresa said, putting her hands on her hips. "We haven't had the discussion, because we're only seeing each other *casually.*"

"All right, all right." Her friend rolled her eyes and called Atticus over to take a slobber-covered stick out of his mouth. "What do you want to talk about, then, if not your supposedly nonexistent love life?"

Theresa eyed the other woman. Grace seemed to genuinely be asking, and she realized her friend wanted a distraction from her worries about her stalker. She relented.

"Liam and I *have* been getting closer." They started walking again, Atticus searching the sand for more interesting items to chew on. "I *do* like him, and as more than just a friend, but I haven't seriously dated for more than twenty years. I'm not sure if I'm ready to."

"But you want to?"

Theresa hesitated. "One day. Not right now, but one day."

It was something she had only recently come to a conclusion on. She didn't want that part of her life to be over forever—being married, having a partner, the sense of sharing her life with someone.

A part of her felt guilty about it, like she should just accept being alone forever because it wasn't fair to Nicolas if she moved on with someone else, but she knew Nicolas would have wanted her to find happiness and love even without him. Her late husband would have been heartbroken if she spent the rest of her life alone and missing him. He had been a good man, and she would be doing him a disservice if she made herself miserable out of some misguided attempt to honor his memory.

"I suppose there's no hurry," Grace said. "It's not like you don't have enough on your plate as it is. Working six days a week would drive me insane."

"I really don't mind it," Theresa said, glad to latch onto an easier subject. "I'll hire more employees eventually and start having at least the option to have more time off, but I enjoy being there." She smiled. "I never would have thought I'd genuinely enjoy working, but it really does make all the difference in the world that it's *my* restaurant. Usually, it barely even feels like work. I'm just there, doing something I want to do, and am lucky enough to get paid for it."

"I was there when you were complaining about all those forms you had to fill out when you hired your employees," Grace pointed out. "I know it's not all sunshine and roses."

Theresa laughed. "That's true. I guess the good parts just make up for the parts that feel like chores."

They walked for a little while longer before turning back and heading toward the apartment. Theresa was glad Grace seemed to be doing all right. They hadn't talked much about her losing her mother, but she hoped her friend knew she was there if she needed someone to listen.

"I was serious when I said you're welcome to take Atticus for an evening if you want," Grace said as they got back to the apartment building. "It's good for him to go out in town and be around other people. I know he gets bored sitting at home with me all the time."

"I might take you up on that," Theresa said. "He's a good—" She broke off as they stepped into the hallway and her eyes found Grace's door. It was partially open. Grace froze next to her, her hands clenching on Atticus's leash.

"I left Molly my keys in case she needed to go somewhere while I was walking," she whispered. "I didn't lock the door behind me when I left. She said she would."

"Maybe she stepped outside for something?" Theresa suggested. They hadn't seen her out front, but there was a grassy area in back she might have gone to for some fresh air.

Grace hesitated, then started walking down the hall. Theresa went with her. When she glanced down at the dog, she saw Atticus had his hackles up.

"Maybe we should—" she started, but Grace was already pushing the door open. She gasped, and Atticus started barking, all the fur along his spine standing up as he backed up into the hall. Theresa looked over her friend's shoulder into the living room.

The place was a mess. The coffee table was over-turned, the couch cushions were on the floor, and lying half across the carpet and half across the linoleum in the kitchen was Molly. Her form was still, there was a small pool of blood under her head. Theresa's stomach clenched.

"Molly," Grace breathed. She dropped Atticus's leash and hurried forward. Theresa grabbed the dog by his collar before he could follow her, some detached part of her mind not wanting him to mess up the evidence. Because, whatever had happened in here, Theresa knew right away it was no accident.

Someone had broken into Grace's apartment while they were on their walk and had killed her friend.

CHAPTER FOUR

"Molly?" Grace knelt by her friend. "Theresa ... she's not moving. I don't know what to do."

Her hands fluttered, as if she was afraid to touch the too-still woman. Atticus was pulling at the end of his leash now, growling and letting out deep, rumbling barks. Theresa wasn't sure she could control him much longer. They needed to call the police, but she didn't have her hands free to reach for her phone.

"Just ... don't move," Theresa said. "I'll go put him in my apartment. I'll be right back."

She pulled Atticus down the hall, unlocked her own door, and pushed the dog inside. She could hear him scrabbling at the other side when she shut the door, but she would worry about the paint later.

She hurried back to the other apartment, where

Grace was still kneeling by her friend. She barely looked up as Theresa took her cell phone out of her purse and shakily dialed the three numbers everyone had drilled into their heads since childhood.

When the dispatcher answered, she told him what they had found as clearly as she could. Following his instructions, she checked Molly for a pulse, which she didn't find, and then carefully guided Grace out of the apartment and into the hallway, keeping her hand on her friend's elbow while the dispatcher told her how soon the police would be there. It didn't seem like it would be quickly enough.

She wondered if shock was something she could get used to. It always happened like this, didn't it? One minute, you were enjoying something simple like a walk with a friend, then the next, everything changed. It had been the same way with Nicolas's cancer diagnosis. A routine doctor's appointment had changed both their lives forever.

She waited with Grace until the police arrived, though the responding officers separated them while they asked questions. Theresa told them everything she could remember, but even so, they finished with her long before they finished talking to Grace. She could hear Atticus barking through the apartment's walls, but no one commented on it; they just raised their voices to talk over the noise.

"Is anything missing?" the detective asked Grace at last, finally having finished with the bulk of his questions. "Any valuables?"

"I don't know," Grace said, looking at the mess of her apartment. "I don't care about valuables. My friend is dead."

"We need to know to help figure out who did this," he told her gently. "If something was taken, the culprit might attempt to sell it at a pawn shop or online. We can have our officers keep an eye out for it."

Grace took a deep breath and started looking around. Finally, her gaze landed on a cookie jar on the counter. The top of it had been thrown off and lay broken on the stove. She walked over and looked at the pieces but didn't touch them.

"I had some money hidden in here," she said. "Taped to the underside of the lid. Just in case."

The detective noted that down. He looked at the cookie jar, at the lid, at the mess of the apartment. "Who knew about that money? Anyone other than you?"

"No," Grace said. Then, "I don't know. I don't think so."

"If you think of someone who does, you let me know," he told her. "If you find that anything else is missing, even if it seems unimportant, let me know."

Grace nodded, but her eyes were far away, like she might not have heard. Theresa resolved to be there for her friend as much as she could because Grace didn't seem to be in any place to take care of herself just then.

Grace couldn't stay at her apartment after that, of course. The police watched her while she grabbed some clothes out of her dresser and snagged some supplies for Atticus, then escorted her out into the hall. They promised they would update her as soon as they were done going through the apartment for evidence, and someone left her a cleaning service's business card, and that was that. Theresa was sure there would be more questioning, more of all of this, at a later date, but for now, Grace was left bereft. Theresa touched her shoulder.

"Let's go into my apartment," she said. "Atticus is worried."

Atticus had scratched up the paint on the inside of her door, but he hadn't done anything else other than knock over one of her chairs. She picked it up, and then turned around to see Grace sitting on the couch, her arms wrapped around her dog's strong neck.

Theresa locked the door and then shot a look at the dining room wall that adjoined Grace's apartment. She could hear the police talking in low murmurs through it.

"What do I do?" Grace asked quietly.

"You can stay here," Theresa offered immediately, even though all she had was a pullout couch.

"I can't," Grace said. "Not knowing what happened right next door. I don't want to have to listen to them. They could be there for hours."

"You could get a motel room." She felt bad even suggesting it. She couldn't just send Grace out there alone to sit in some dingy motel room right after her friend was murdered. Quickly, she amended, "I don't really want to stay here tonight either. We can get motel rooms together, adjoining ones. That place just south of town allows dogs, don't they?"

Grace wiped at her eyes and nodded. Theresa picked up her phone again, searched the name of the motel, and called the front desk. She paid for both of the rooms over the phone and then started packing her bags.

The motel was one of the worst ones Theresa had ever stayed in. It looked like it had been old since even before Jace was born, and she was pretty sure the carpet wasn't supposed to be that dingy brown color. But it was the first place she could think of that she knew wouldn't make a big deal about Atticus. She wasn't sure what breed he was, but with his big, blocky head, his short fur, and his broad muzzle, he looked like a pit bull or some sort of large, bull breed mix, and she knew Grace had had problems finding places to stay with him before.

When she checked in, no one even asked what breed their dog was, they just handed her the key cards and told her when checkout was. She had made sure they had adjoining rooms, and she told Grace just to knock if she wanted company. Then she sat down on the bed in her own sad, dingy motel room and looked at the stained walls. This was hardly where she had thought she would be spending her evening. If it was just her, she would have gone to her cousin's house instead, but she wouldn't have felt right about asking Clare to put up a woman she barely knew, and she didn't want to just leave Grace alone.

She decided to let Clare know what was going on, at least. She called her, and her cousin answered with a cheerful, "Hey, lady. Want to hit the beach with me soon?"

"Something happened," Theresa said, feeling bad about wrecking her good mood.

"What's wrong? Is Jace okay?" Clare's voice became low and serious immediately.

"He's fine," Theresa said. She heard her cousin sigh with relief on the other end of the line. "It's my neighbor, Grace. Remember her?"

Quietly, she told Clare about Grace's stalker, about the man she had seen outside the apartment building, and then about the horrible, violent discovery they had stumbled across when they got back from walking Atticus that afternoon.

Clare was both shocked and horrified. "It's times like this when I wish I really *was* a psychic," she said. "I wish I could help. That poor woman. Poor *you*. How do you keep getting involved in this sort of thing, Theresa?"

"It's not like I try to," Theresa muttered. "I just want to help—" She broke off as a knock sounded at the room's adjoining door. "I've got to go; I think Grace wants to talk to me. I'll call you back later."

She said a quick goodbye and hung up the phone, then went to open her door. Atticus came rushing into her room, sniffing around it as if it was the most inter-esting thing in the world, despite the fact that it was a mirrored copy of Grace's room. His owner followed him more slowly, her eyes red rimmed, though she wasn't actively crying at the moment.

"I need to talk to you," Grace said, her voice a lot firmer than Theresa expected. "I haven't been completely truthful. I don't know *who's* stalking me, and I don't know who broke into my apartment and killed Molly, but I do know *why*."

CHAPTER FIVE

Theresa sat on the edge of her bed. Grace sat on the uncomfortable wooden chair in front of the room's tiny excuse for a desk. She looked down at her nails, picking her cuticles. Finally, she took a deep breath.

"My mom was … well off. Wealthy."

Theresa hadn't known what to expect, but it hadn't been that. She didn't know how this tied into what happened to Molly yet, but she nodded at her friend to go on. Grace did, but only after a second.

"Her health was really bad at the end, but she was still all there mentally. She was still her, you know?" Grace looked at her uncertainly, so Theresa nodded. Her friend continued, "She and my sister had a really bad relationship. I don't want to get into the details much, but they both thought they had valid reasons for how they felt about each other. I tried to stay out of it, but I ended up being a lot closer with my mom than my sister. I still love her, but… She just wasn't really close with us. She ended up being closer with my dad's side of the family, who my mom had a bad falling out with and I rarely see."

"That sounds like a hard situation to be in," Theresa said. She didn't have any siblings, but had always wanted one, and didn't imagine it would feel good to be estranged from someone you had grown up with.

Grace nodded. "That's just background information. I wanted you to understand a little bit about my family dynamics when I told you my mom deposited a little bit over one million dollars into my bank account a few days before she died."

Theresa stared at her friend. "Is that … legal?" She had a lot of other questions but didn't know what to ask first.

"We went to a bank. She had to fill out a gift form, and I guess I'll have to file it in my taxes next year, but … yes?" Grace looked like she was a little stunned by it all still. "She wanted to leave me the bulk of her money, and she didn't want to risk anyone challenging the will to get it from her. She still left something for my sister, but it's not anywhere near as much. She explained it all in a letter along with her will. She had been planning to do it for a while—the letter was dated a few months ago."

"So, you think this had something to do with what happened to Molly?"

"I'm almost sure it did," Grace said. "My sister and my dad's family would know all about it by now. The stalking didn't start until after I got back from attending my mother's funeral and will reading. It has to be related."

"So, your sister is the one behind it?"

Grace bit her lip. "I don't know. It could be my dad. They were divorced, but if he heard about it, he might be thinking he could get some money from me. Or ... well, I didn't think much of it at the time, but about a week ago, my ex called and started acting like he was trying to get back together with me. I haven't exactly been in the mood to date, so I just told him I wasn't interested in going out and left it at that, but now I'm wondering... If he somehow learned I had that money, maybe it was him. He started acting very oddly after he learned how well off my mother was. It was one of the reasons I broke up with him."

"Have you told the police all of this?" Theresa asked.

"I mentioned a large inheritance briefly when they

questioned me at the apartment," Grace said. "I didn't go into much detail, but I mentioned the money and the fact that the rest of my family wasn't happy about it."

"What does your sister look like?" Theresa asked. It seemed a long time ago now, but she remembered the woman she had overheard on the phone at the crêperie earlier that same day.

"Monica? She looks a lot like me, a little taller. Similar hair."

"I thought I was just being paranoid, but today someone came into the crêperie who looked a lot like you described. And she was talking to someone on the phone and said your name."

Grace's eyes widened. "My sister is here? In town?"

"I'll check the receipts tomorrow to be sure," Theresa offered. "She paid with her card, so the receipt from her order should have her name on it."

"Please do," Grace said. "I can't imagine her doing something so violent like—like what happened today—but I definitely can imagine her being behind everything else. I bet she hired that man you saw in the parking lot. She must have been scoping out where I lived before she came to town."

Grace rose to her feet and started pacing back and

forth across the motel room floor. Atticus jumped onto the bed beside Theresa and lay down with a groan. Theresa watched Grace pace and wished she knew what to say to help her friend feel better.

They ordered cheap pizza for dinner. Neither of them were very hungry, but they both forced down a slice or two. Grace sat at the table, picking pieces of pepperoni off the top of the pizza and tossing them to Atticus, who was having the time of his life now, his earlier upset at the apartment forgotten.

Grace retreated to her own motel room after that, and Theresa picked up her phone again to call her son, who would want to know what was going on. After that, she called Clare back and chatted with her cousin until dark.

Theresa felt bad leaving Grace alone the next day. She offered to call off work, but Grace told her she could take care of herself. "I need to go to the police station anyway. I want to tell them more about everything that happened while I was visiting my mom. You should act normal—if someone really is following me, we don't want to give them any reason to involve you in this."

Grace made a good point, so Theresa went into work and did her best to pretend everything was normal. She chopped up her ingredients, smiled at her customers, and as far as she could tell, she didn't slip once until she looked out the window onto Main Street and saw a man sitting in a tan car out on the curb.

She recognized the man. She recognized the car. She stared at him until the customer she was making a crêpe for said, "Um, I think you're burning it." Then she looked down and realized she was going to have to start the order from scratch.

She was shaking as she tried to finish the order. She was absolutely certain that was the same man she'd seen at her apartment building on Monday. She didn't know what to do. Should she call the police? Would they take her seriously if she said, *"Yeah, there's a man sitting outside my restaurant, and I saw him sitting outside my apartment the day before yesterday too. Just wanted to let you know."*

She thought they might, given what happened to Molly. As soon as she had a moment, she would make the call. Kian was in the back, making more chicken for their very popular chicken pesto crêpes, and there was a line at the register. It was a busy day, almost frustratingly so. Normally, she liked the busy days, but not when she was worried about her friend and still reeling from stumbling onto a murder scene.

She moved over to the register to take the next

person's order. She barely glanced at him, doing her job almost on autopilot. "Welcome to the Crooked Crêperie. What can I get for you today?"

"What's crème fraiche?"

"It's a little like a cross between sour cream and heavy cream," she explained. "It's not as tangy as sour cream. We make it ourselves. If you'd like to try some, I can get you a sample."

"No, that's okay. It sounds good. I'll take your special," the man said. While she was ringing it up, he spoke again. "You're Grace's neighbor, aren't you?"

Theresa froze. "I'm sorry, do I know you?"

"I might have seen you before. Grace and I were dating up until earlier this year. How is she doing? I heard something happened at the apartment building yesterday."

"I'm sorry, but I'm not comfortable talking about that," Theresa said. She was hoping he couldn't tell how quickly her heart was pounding. She typed the rest of the order in. "Will that be cash or card?"

He handed her a twenty. While she made change, he said, "I'm Brandon. Brandon Miller. She might have said something about me."

"Sorry, I don't think I can help you," Theresa said. She handed him his change and moved over to the griddle. "Will that be for here or to go?"

"To go," he said, though he didn't sound happy about it.

Thankfully, he left once he got his food. By the time she looked out the window again, the man in the car had left too, but she didn't think they had gone away together. She'd seen Brandon walk away down the sidewalk, at least, so if they were working together, they were trying to keep it quiet.

As soon as she had a moment to step into the kitchen and ask Kian to cover the register, she took her phone out of her pocket and called Grace's number. Her friend had already mentioned her ex once in relation to Molly's murder. She needed to know about this as soon as possible.

CHAPTER SIX

Grace didn't answer her call, but she did text back to say she was busy but wanted to meet later. Theresa wasn't sure where to offer to meet her. She needed to go back to her own apartment for a change of clothes, but she didn't want to ask Grace to meet her there in case she wasn't ready to return to the apartment building yet.

After a moment, she called Liam. He was at work, but he owned a used bookstore that was rarely busy, so it wasn't unusual that he answered sounding ready to chat. She realized he didn't know about Molly or anything that was going on with Grace, so she filled him in on the basics—skipping over the parts about the money and Grace's family—then asked him for a favor.

"I want to meet Grace somewhere she feels safe. Can we use the back room at your bookstore? She'll have Atticus with her."

"Of course the three of you can use the back room," he said, agreeing without hesitation. "I wish I'd known sooner. I'm sorry this happened. Do you want me to order a late lunch for you and Grace? I was thinking of ordering out anyway. I know it's not much, but…"

"I appreciate the offer, but I can pick something up. How does Club King sound? Text me your order. And don't argue, just consider it thanks for giving up your back room for a few hours."

He chuckled. "All right. I hope you know you're welcome to come here whenever you need to, though."

She did know that, and the thought put a warm feeling in her chest despite everything else. She thanked him, said her goodbyes, and ended the call. Then, she texted Grace the plan.

It wasn't until she was waiting in line at Club King, a deli just down the road from the crêperie that boasted some truly delicious sandwiches, that she remembered the double date she and Liam were supposed to have with Clare and Clare's boyfriend, Afton, tonight.

She'd have to cancel it. Some mysteries were just more important than dinner.

She arrived at the bookstore at almost the same time Grace did. She paused outside to greet her and Atticus, carefully lifting the bag with their sandwiches in it away from his questing nose. There wasn't anyone beside Liam inside when they entered the building, and she felt more relaxed as she walked through the crowded aisles of books—even though his organizational system still made her cringe.

Who organized an entire bookstore alphabetically by author name, not even by subject or genre?

Liam came out from behind the counter to give her a hug. Atticus was so thrilled to see him that he pulled the leash out of Grace's hand. Liam ducked to grab the leash and greeted the exuberant dog.

"I'm very sorry to hear about what happened, Grace," he said once Atticus was a little calmer. "You are welcome to spend as long as you need here. I'm going to keep the place open until six, but even after I close, the two of you are welcome to stay as long as you want." He gave Theresa a questioning look, and she thought he was probably wondering about their date.

"Let me show you where the back room is," she

said to her friend. "Then I'm going to come back out here and talk to Liam for a second."

She left Grace in the back room with Atticus and the bag of sandwiches and returned to the front, stepping behind the counter to join Liam at his spot near the register. She eyed the ancient machine; she'd had a hard enough time figuring her modern register out.

"I'm going to call Clare and cancel the date," she said after a second. "I feel bad doing it, but Grace shouldn't be alone right now."

"Clare will understand," Liam said.

"She's going to be disappointed. You know how excited she always gets about going out with Afton."

"Why don't you invite them over here?" he suggested. "We can get takeout, have a night in. Not a date, just a meal and some time spent with friends. Grace knows Clare, right?"

"They've met, but they don't know each other well." Theresa considered the idea. "I'll ask her. She might want the distraction, or she might not want to be around anyone. Either way, I'll let her choose."

When she rejoined Grace in the back room, her friend was picking at her sandwich, and Atticus was staring at her, ready to snatch it if she dropped any part of it.

Theresa took a chair across from her. "How are you doing?"

Grace shrugged. "I just feel lost, I guess. I don't really know what to do. Atticus and I went to the police station today, then we drove around for a while, just trying to keep occupied. The police don't want me to go home yet. I'll probably stay at a motel again tonight."

Theresa wished she had a place to offer Grace to stay that wasn't the apartment right next door to where her friend had been murdered. The motel had been depressing.

She was on the verge of deciding to just cancel with Clare after all when Grace looked up at her with a frown. "Didn't you have plans for tonight? You told me about it last week. A date with Liam and your cousin and that guy she's seeing?"

"It's not important," Theresa said.

"Don't say that. I've dragged you into all of this with me already. How can I ask you to miss a date on top of that?"

"Really, Grace, it's nothing."

"No, you have to go."

Theresa hesitated. "Well, Liam and I were thinking … maybe we could invite them here? You've met Clare, and Afton is a nice guy. I don't know if the extra company would be welcome or not. Either way is fine with me, honestly. I see my cousin all the time."

"I think you should have them over." Grace slid her sandwich closer and took a bite of it. "I think being around people will help. I just don't want to be alone right now. Every time I am, I feel like someone's watching me. It will make me less nervous to have more people around."

Theresa hesitated, but she could understand where Grace was coming from. "All right. Let me give my cousin a call, then I'll tell you about everything that happened today."

Clare and Afton agreed to the change of plans. It would be a few hours before they got there with the food, so Theresa sat down with Grace and ate half her sandwich as she told the other woman about the man in the tan car outside the crêperie and the unsettling interaction with Brandon Miller.

"I knew it," Grace said when she finished. "He has to know about the money. There's no other reason he would be asking about me. Our breakup was very final."

"You told the police about him, right?" Theresa asked. "If he had something to do with Molly, they'll figure it out. You just have to avoid him until then."

"How long will it take, though?" Grace asked. "He's obviously trying to figure out where I am, if he's asking you about me. I may not be safe anywhere."

"Well, he won't learn where you are from me," Theresa promised. Hoping to lighten the mood a little, she said, "And you've got Atticus. He's a good boy. He won't let anything happen to you."

The dog looked up at the sound of his name, and his tail thumped against the floor. Grace stroked his head. "I wish my mother had never given me that money."

Theresa didn't know what to say to that, so she didn't say anything at all.

Since Afton was the only one of them who didn't know what had happened to Grace's friend, Grace agreed that they should fill him in when they got there —at least, about what had happened to Molly and the stalking. The rest she wanted to keep between Theresa and her.

The dinner turned into an impromptu brainstorming session, but the food was good—Afton had brought it from one of his restaurants—and Grace seemed to be a little more relaxed by the end of it. Theresa hoped the distraction had helped her feel better, even if just for a few hours. It wasn't until

Clare and Afton were leaving the bookstore later that night that Theresa realized she still didn't know where she was going to go herself. If Grace was getting her own motel room, Theresa supposed she would go back to her apartment alone, even though the thought made her uncomfortable. Someone had been murdered on the other side of her dining room wall, for goodness' sake. Grace must have been worrying about the same thing because after all their goodbyes were said and Clare and Afton drove away, she seemed to wilt.

"I hate that I can't even go home. I don't even know if I *want* to go home. It's not fair that I can't feel safe in my own home."

"Why don't you stay here?" Liam asked. "Both of you. There's a guest bedroom and also a pullout couch. Plenty of space—I'll be in my room all night and will stay out of your hair. I don't think anyone would guess you're here, unless they followed you here earlier, so it should be safe."

Liam lived above the bookstore, in the top half of the old house it occupied. Theresa met his eyes and smiled at him while Grace considered the offer.

"Are you sure? I don't want to inconvenience you."

"It's not an inconvenience at all," Liam assured

her. "Just give me a second to tidy up, then you're welcome to come up."

"Thank you," Theresa said. She meant it. She hadn't been so grateful to someone in a long time. "I'll stay too, of course. We appreciate it."

They decided to take Atticus out back while Liam tidied up above their heads. The bookstore was in a more residential part of town and had a small, fenced yard behind it. Grace let Atticus off his leash and watched him start sniffing every inch of the yard.

"I hate feeling like such a burd—" Grace started, but she fell silent at the musical notes of her phone's ringtone. She fumbled through her purse for it and brought it out, then stared at the screen.

"Who is it?" Theresa asked, already sure it couldn't be anything good.

"It … it's my sister."

She answered the phone as if in a daze and brought it to her ear. "Monica?"

Theresa couldn't hear what the other woman was saying. She waited on tenterhooks, watching Grace's face for any sign of what was happening.

"I don't know if that's a…" She trailed off. "Yes, I know you came all the way out here just to see me. I have something going on…" She sighed as the woman on the other end of the call kept talking.

"Fine, but it has to be somewhere public, at least." She glanced at Theresa. "There's a crêpe restaurant—you know it? All right. I'll see you there tomorrow, I guess."

She ended the call, then turned to look at Theresa. "My sister wants to meet me tomorrow. I didn't know what else to say, she wasn't taking no for an answer. I hope it's okay I told her we'd meet at the crêperie. She's coming at noon, so there should be plenty of other people around. Even if she's involved in what happened to Molly, nothing should happen when we meet tomorrow."

It sounded like a horrible idea to Theresa, but what was done was done. If Monica really was behind this, canceling might only make things worse. They would just have to be cautious and smart.

CHAPTER SEVEN

Theresa slept better at Liam's house than she did at the motel. She told Grace to take the guest room with Atticus and slept on the pullout couch. It was old and much less comfortable than her own was, but at least she didn't have to worry about the last time the sheets had been washed, which was a thought that had kept her up in the motel.

It was very strange to wake up to the sound of Liam moving around in the kitchen while he made coffee. It was a little awkward to see him first thing in the morning like this, but by the time Grace woke up, they were sitting at his small kitchen table chatting about their plans to visit Afton's lake house with Clare sometime in the next couple of weeks. Once

Grace joined them, looking very tired this early in the morning, the topic changed to her upcoming meeting with her sister.

"I still don't think it's a good idea," Liam said. He'd been against the plan since they told him about it the night before. "You yourself said she's the most likely culprit behind all of this."

"She's my sister, though," Grace said. "I'm not close to her, but she's still my family. I just... I have to give her a chance. I'm her big sister. Theresa is going to have the police on speed dial in case anything happens, and we are meeting in a public place. I don't see what she could be planning."

He frowned, then said, "If you want an extra set of friendly eyes at the crêperie while you're meeting her, I can close the bookshop for lunch a little early."

His lack of commitment to keeping regular hours at the bookstore was another small quirk of his that normally drove Theresa crazy, but she found that she didn't mind it so much this time. "If it's not any trouble, I'd appreciate that." She glanced at Grace. "I really *would* prefer that nothing goes wrong today."

At least they had a plan when they left Liam's house that morning. Grace was going to drive around and find a crowded place to have breakfast in the next town over while Theresa swung by her apartment and got ready for work. She hadn't been back since the day of the murder, but she hadn't thought very far ahead when she hurriedly packed an overnight bag. She needed a change of clothes and a decent shower before going to work.

There was still crime scene tape on Grace's door when she entered the building. Her own door was locked, just as she'd left it, but she was still cautious as she opened it and stepped into her apartment. She turned the deadbolt behind her and glanced at the scratched paint. She really would have to repair that. She wasn't upset with Atticus—he had been upset and had reacted in the only way he knew how—but she didn't want to get charged for the damage either.

She moved through her apartment quietly, checking in the closet and under the bed even though she felt a little silly about doing so. Everything that was going on with Grace had spooked her. At least one person—Brandon—had already asked her about Grace. She had no idea if he was involved in the murder yet, but if one person knew she was Grace's neighbor and friend, then other people might too. She was determined to stand with the other woman, but it didn't mean she wanted to become a target herself.

After reassuring herself that she was the only one in her apartment, she took a quick shower and hurried to get ready for work on time. They had gotten up painfully early, but she was going to be cutting it close anyway. She didn't want to be late today. She didn't want to do anything that might alert the killer that she was involved.

It was only after she got to the crêperie and Wynne clocked in with a cheerful greeting and chatter about the upcoming day that she realized a flaw in their plan. It was unfair of her to expose her employee to someone who might be involved with a murder, especially when Wynne had no idea what was going on and had no say in the matter.

She didn't settle on a solution until it was nearly time for Grace to arrive. Monica was supposed to arrive at noon—so, right at lunchtime. As much as Theresa loved eating and making crêpes, eating the same thing every day would bore almost anyone. It wasn't unheard of for her to call out for pickup or delivery if she had skipped an early breakfast, and she realized that gave her the perfect excuse to get Wynne safely out of the restaurant while Monica was there.

Theresa called a pickup order in to Meat at the Bay, and then asked Wynne to go pick it up. Wynne was glad for the chance to get out of the restaurant for a bit, especially on such a nice summer day, and left just as Grace pulled up outside the restaurant.

Grace glanced at Theresa as she came in, but she walked over to her table without greeting her. They had agreed on that—if someone was watching, they didn't want it obvious that Grace knew her. Theresa busied herself with cleaning the counter by the register, trying not to seem like she was watching the door.

Liam was the next to arrive. Theresa and her crêperie were well enough known around town that anyone who enjoyed gossip would know she was friends and maybe more with Liam Shaw, so he made no pretense of not knowing her when he came in. He came up to the counter and ordered a crêpe— one of the breakfast ones, with eggs and bacon and cheese—and then started talking about a rare book show he was planning on going to in a couple of months. She tried to listen, or tried to at least look like she was listening, but it was hard because her eyes kept going back to the door even as she made his crêpe.

Monica came in just as she was plating it. Theresa didn't know what it meant that she was late, or if it even meant anything at all, but she *did* immediately know that this was the same woman who had come in the day of the murder. The similarities between her and Grace were more evident now that she knew they were related.

She spotted her sister right away, and though her lips tightened, she didn't go over to her at first. She turned to the counter and waited for Theresa to finish handing Liam his crêpe. He took it to an empty table not far from where Grace was sitting while she took Monica's order.

"I'd like to try one of your chicken pesto crêpes this time," she said before Theresa could even greet her. "For here, please."

"Coming right up," Theresa said, hoping she sounded chipper and not as stressed as she felt.

She got the crêpe made more out of muscle memory than anything, plated it, and then watched as Monica walked across the room to join her sister at the table. She was too far away to hear what they were saying, but Liam glanced up and waved her over as if he needed something, and she was glad to take the opportunity to drift a little closer to the conversation.

"… not hungry," Grace was saying. "Just say what you came here to say, Monica. Why did you fly across the country to see me?"

"You know why," Monica said. "I'm going to be contesting the will and how our mother's assets were dispersed. I want to give you a chance to do what's right first."

"How did you even find me?"

"I have my ways," Monica said. "I'm not even asking for half of it. Just … something."

"You already got something. She left us equal amounts in her will."

"You and I both know she had a lot more money than that," Monica retorted. "I know about the transfer she made to you, Grace. It can't be legal. We're both her daughters. We deserve an equal share."

"I haven't decided what I'm doing yet," Grace said. "It's too much for me to even think about right now. If you just came here to ask me to give you money, the answer is no. At least, not right now. I need to figure some stuff out first."

"I'm not going to let this rest," Monica insisted. "So don't get too comfortable." She looked around, frowning at Theresa and Liam.

Theresa pretended she needed to refill Liam's glass of water, and in doing so, she missed the rest of the conversation. When she returned, Grace was just sitting there, and Monica was eating her crêpe in silence. Theresa returned to the counter and took the next order, though she kept looking over at their table every chance she got.

It wasn't until a loud group of pedestrians walked past the crêperie's window and Theresa glanced their way reflexively that she saw it. The car across the street. Slowly, carefully, she took her phone out under the counter and texted Liam.

The tan car across the street. There's a man in it, the same man I saw at the apartment building. I think he's the one who has been stalking Grace.

She sent the text and waited until she saw Liam take his phone out of his pocket. He gave no response to her text, just slipped his phone back into his pocket. After a moment, he ate the last few bites of his crêpe and got up and headed out the door, pausing to send a casual wave goodbye in her direction. She waved back, trying to match how unconcerned he looked, and kept her eyes on him as he crossed the street and approached the tan vehicle. It wasn't until he was almost at the driver's side window that the person inside seemed to realize he had been spotted.

Just like when she met his eyes in her rearview mirror in the apartment parking lot, he pulled away immediately. Liam fumbled his phone out of his pocket and raised it to take a picture of the car as it was leaving, but she didn't know how successful he was.

At Grace's table, Monica stood up.

"I'd better get going. We're not done talking yet, Grace. I'd rather figure something out between the two of us than spend the money fighting you in a long, drawn-out legal battle. I'll give you a call in a day or two. I hope you change your mind by then."

CHAPTER EIGHT

Grace stayed until she was sure her sister was gone, then went up to the counter to talk to Theresa. There was a small line at the register by then, and Theresa had to force herself to act like everything was normal until she could finally talk to her friend.

"I'm going to go talk to the detective again," Grace told her once they had a chance to speak semi-privately. "I'm going to tell him about my meeting with her."

"Do you think she had something to do with what happened to Molly?" Theresa asked.

Grace frowned. "I don't know. In a lot of ways, it makes sense. She was a hair away from threatening me for the money, you heard her. But … what was the point of killing my friend or breaking into my apartment? She knows I'm not keeping a million dollars cash in my apartment. She mentioned involving lawyers, too. I don't think she would do that if she committed a crime herself."

"That's a good point," Theresa admitted. "Maybe the lawyers were an empty threat? She might be trying to scare you into giving the money up."

"If she was doing that, then she'd make it clearer she was threatening me, though, wouldn't she?" Grace shook her head. "Either way, thank you for letting me meet her here. And thank Liam too, when you see him. Why did he leave so suddenly like that?"

"Did you see that car he was walking toward?" Theresa asked. Grace nodded. "That's the same car I saw at the apartment building and then here in front of the crêperie yesterday. The same man has been watching from inside it each time."

Grace glanced outside, but the car was long gone. "Did he get the license plate number? Or did the security cameras?"

"The security cameras only see the sidewalk right in front of the store, they wouldn't have seen across the street. But Liam might have gotten a picture. He tried, but I don't know if he was fast enough. Hold on, let me check my phone."

She pulled out her phone and sure enough, he had

already texted her an image. It was a blurry photo of the tan car driving away, the license plate nothing but a smudge of white and blue. She showed it to Grace, who sighed.

"Send it to me anyway, maybe the police can do something with it. This is so stressful, Theresa. I feel like I've barely even had time to mourn Molly. I've just been so worried every single second since she dicd."

"I'm sorry," Theresa told her. "I wish there was more I could do to help you."

"You've done so much already. I'll just have to keep marching on."

Theresa offered her a free crêpe for lunch, but Grace waved her off and promised she would eat something later. Theresa watched her go, feeling like she wasn't doing enough, despite Grace's words.

Her friend texted her an hour later with the news that she'd finally gotten the all clear to go back to her apartment, and that the cleaning crew would be done by four. Theresa agreed to meet her there after work, and they would go in together.

She kept her eyes peeled for that tan car and its mysterious driver during the remainder of her shift, but she didn't see it again. In fact, the rest of the day was about as average as it got. No one came in asking for Grace, no one watched through the windows. It was a pleasant slice of normalcy. She did her best to enjoy the expensive barbecue she had ordered when Wynne got back with it and forced herself not to hurry when three o'clock rolled around and she started closing. She wasn't supposed to meet Grace until four anyway—it wasn't like she would be late even if she took twice as long as she normally did.

As she drove back to her apartment, she wondered if Grace would be able to return to living and sleeping and eating there as if nothing had ever happened. She couldn't imagine doing so herself, but she also didn't know what else the other woman could do. She probably couldn't afford to move without notice—

But, she could. Theresa hadn't actually stopped to consider the fact that Grace had been gifted a significant sum of money. It was a huge change for Grace. The circumstances surrounding the money were horrible, but she hoped that one day, that money would make her friend's life easier.

Grace was already waiting in the parking lot when Theresa showed up. Her eyes scanned the lot automatically for any out-of-place cars, but there weren't any. Most of the other tenants of the building were still at work, so it was just her car, Grace's car, and the old sedan that belonged to the elderly man who lived in one of the upstairs units. Anything unfamiliar would have stood out like a sore thumb.

Grace got out of her car as soon as Theresa parked. Atticus seemed happy to be back at the apartment building and started pulling toward the door. Grace held him back, struggling with the leash until he saw Theresa and changed directions toward her. She patted the dog, then looked over at her friend.

"Are you ready to go in?"

"As ready as I'll ever be," Grace said.

Theresa had been here once since the murder, but this was the first time Grace had returned. Theresa went first, pulling the door into the hallway open and stepping into the building. Grace hesitated for a second before following. Once they were inside, Atticus led the way, pulling down the hall all the way to the door of the apartment that had been his home for years. He pawed at it, his tail hitting Theresa in the legs.

Grace took her keys out of her purse and unlocked her door. Theresa could smell the sharp, lemon scent of cleaner before they even went inside. The place had been tidied up enough that she wouldn't have known what happened if she hadn't seen it with her own eyes. Grace looked around the living room for a second, then unclipped Atticus's leash. The dog started sniffing around the room, evidently fascinated by all the new smells.

"Well, I'm home," Grace said, her voice flat.

"I'll be right next door," Theresa reminded her. "You're welcome to come over at any time. Just knock."

Grace nodded. Theresa backed out of the apartment, pulled the door gently shut, and then returned to her own apartment. She unlocked the door and stepped inside, trying and failing to feel the sense of comfort being home was supposed to bring her. She could see the parking lot from her patio door. Normally, her eyes were drawn to the bay behind it, but right now all she could think of was that tan car. It wasn't there now, but as she watched, a vehicle she didn't recognize pulled in.

It was an old black truck, and she could see a dark-haired man in the driver's seat. The sight made her freeze. Had the mystery man in the tan car gotten a different vehicle?

It wasn't until he stepped out of the truck that she realized this was no mystery man. It was Brandon, Grace's ex.

This was not good. She backed away from the patio window and hurried toward her door, pulling it open and rushing back down the hall toward Grace's apartment to knock frantically at the same door she had shut behind her just a few moments ago. Grace opened it a second later, looking at her in shock.

"Theresa, what is it? What happened?"

"Brandon's here," she said. "He just pulled into the parking lot."

Grace's eyes widened. She beckoned Theresa in and shut the door behind her just as Theresa heard the door at the end of the hall open.

CHAPTER NINE

Brandon knocked on Grace's apartment door a few seconds later. Atticus started letting out his big, booming barks. Grace grabbed his collar to stop him from jumping up at the door, but the dog was loud enough they could barely hear Brandon when he started speaking.

"I know you're in there, Grace. I saw your car in the parking lot. I just want to check on you. I'm trying to make sure you're okay after everything that happened."

Theresa glanced over at Grace. Her friend had her lips pressed shut and raised a finger to them. Theresa nodded. Brandon might have seen her go into the apartment as he entered the building, but he might not have. There was no point in letting him know for certain someone was inside.

He pounded on the door again. "I know something is going on. The police came and talked to me yesterday. I'm worried about you. I wish you would at least let me see that you are all right." They remained silent. Finally, his fist gave a single last thud on the door. "Grace! Answer me." He tried the doorknob, and Theresa tensed. The door was locked, but it was still unsettling to hear the doorknob rattle as he tried to get in.

Then, they heard another, muffled voice on the other side of the door. The newcomer was saying something to Brandon, and though he knocked one last time after that, he finally fell silent for long enough Theresa thought he might have left. After a few moments, she moved forward to check the peephole. She jumped a little when she saw a face peering back at her, but it wasn't Brandon—this was someone she recognized, the new neighbor who had moved in across from Grace. The woman looked like she was about to knock, and Theresa opened the door before the sound could set Atticus off again. Grace made a noise of protest behind her, but Theresa only opened the door a couple of inches, making sure to block the rest of the apartment with her body. A glance down the hall showed her Brandon was gone.

"Oh—Theresa, right?" the older woman said. She and her husband mostly kept to themselves, but they had introduced themselves to everyone in the building when they first moved in.

Theresa nodded. "Hi, Vivi. How can I help you?"

"I saw that man pounding on the door, and I heard the dog barking. I figured if Grace wasn't answering, she didn't want to see him. He told me he was a friend of hers, but I told him if he kept causing a disturbance, I would report him, and he finally left. Is everything all right?"

Grace tapped her on the shoulder, so Theresa stepped aside. "We're fine, Vivi. Thank you for stepping in. He's my ex, and I was trying to avoid him, so I appreciate it."

"This doesn't have anything to do with that..." The older woman lowered her voice. "...nasty business with the police, does it? Mark and I heard about what happened, and we were just horrified. Especially knowing the history of our own unit. This building just doesn't have any luck, does it? How are you holding up?"

"I'm getting by," Grace said. She glanced toward

the main door. "I'll catch you up on things later, Vivi. Can you let me know if you see him around again?"

"Of course. I'll tell Mark to keep an eye out for him too."

Theresa and Grace said their goodbyes and then retreated back into Grace's apartment, locking the door behind them once again. Grace sat on the couch, putting her head in her hands. "I wish everyone would just leave me alone." Atticus nudged her elbow, and she sat up a little to pet him, then glanced at Theresa. "Not you, of course. But Brandon, my sister, whoever that guy in the car is who has been following me... Oh, Theresa. You shouldn't even be helping me. Look at what happened to Molly. She came all the way out here just to stay with me, and someone killed her for it. I should just get out of town and try to disappear for a while, while the police work on solving her murder."

"If your sister really *did* hire someone to follow you, they might be able to track you down even if you're careful," Theresa pointed out, worried. "You would be in even more danger if you were out there alone. I know the risks, but you're my friend, and I want to help you. I can't in good conscience just walk away from this. Liam is offering his help too, even though he barely knows you. You've got Atticus—

he's not going to let anyone hurt you. It will be all right."

"It just feels so hopeless."

"We'll keep trying to figure out who's behind this. Do you want to call that detective who's working on your case and tell him that Brandon came here?"

"What would the point be?" Grace asked. "It's not illegal for him to knock on my door and check up on me. He wasn't even harassing me, really. It's not like I asked him to leave. The only reason I even think he *might* be involved with all of this is how soon he contacted me after that money entered my account. I don't know, Theresa. I'm just … tired. I want Molly's killer to be caught, and I want whoever is behind all of this to leave me alone."

Theresa stood there, her hands on her hips, looking at her friend. Grace was the first friend she'd made in years who wasn't related to her and who wasn't a coworker, and even though she and the other woman had an age difference and completely different experiences in life, they had grown close. She hated the fact that Grace was so upset and there was nothing she could do. It made her feel like a bad friend.

"I'm going to call off work tomorrow," she decided. Grace looked up, ready to object, but

Theresa pressed on. "Kian has been asking for more hours anyway. You and I will spend the day out of town doing something fun. We can go on a hike with Atticus, maybe. Explore some of the surrounding towns, go out to eat. We're going to get away from all this, even if just for a little while. You need to distract yourself, Grace. You haven't been thinking about anything except what happened for days now. I think a little space will do you good."

She arranged things with Kian, who seemed happy enough to take over her weekend hours, and sat with Grace for a little while until her friend was no longer worried that Brandon was going to show back up. After that, Theresa returned to her own apartment, which she had barely spent any time in all week. It needed a good dusting, so she did that, then she called Jace and talked to him on speakerphone while she cleaned out her fridge.

He was worried, since she had gotten involved with something dangerous again. She hated worrying him, but she had promised him to keep him in the loop, and she intended to keep that promise. He was her son, but he was also an adult, and she understood the need to know what was going on in the life of someone you loved.

It felt surprisingly good to fall asleep in her own

bed that night. She hoped Grace was readjusting to being home well too. She knew it would be harder for her, but hopefully, her apartment would become a haven again.

Theresa felt a little guilty about sleeping in the next morning, but she knew Grace wouldn't be up at the crack of dawn, and there was no reason for her to set her alarm if she wasn't going into the crêperie. By the time she woke up, the sun was shining, and the news, which she listened to as she made coffee, promised a pleasant day. It was supposed to be partially cloudy with a light breeze that would keep the temperature down, and no threat of rain until after dark. The perfect day for a hike, in other words.

She and Grace didn't end up leaving until almost noon. Grace looked tired, as if she hadn't slept well, but as the three of them piled into Theresa's car, Atticus in the back with his head out the window, she forced a smile.

"It will be good to get out and do something active. Thank you for doing all this, Theresa. You are a good friend."

"I try to be," Theresa said. "Can you navigate? I know roughly how to get there, but I'll need directions when we get closer."

They were going to a state forest about half an

hour away. Neither of them had been there before, and it was far enough away from town that she didn't think anyone who might be looking for Grace would stumble upon them accidentally. She was a little worried about someone following them out there, but as soon as they left town and started down one of the country roads, it became evident that no one was on their tail. Grace seemed to breathe a little easier at the sight of the empty road.

When they arrived at the park, they decided to hike a four-mile loop through the woods. Atticus was happy enough to be out there that it made even Grace give a genuine smile, and though Theresa was a little concerned that someone might be waiting for them when they got back to the car, nothing happened. There was no sign anyone had followed them.

They were hungry after their hike, so they went to the closest town and found a tiny diner, where they ordered takeout and ate the food in the car with Atticus. If it wasn't for the circumstances of *why* they had wanted to get out of town, it would have been a perfect day.

It was late afternoon, almost evening by the time they headed back home. The day spent hiking had been freeing, but as she turned onto the last stretch of road before they reached the apartment building, she felt her good mood start to drain away.

What would they do if they got back and Brandon's truck or the mysterious man in the tan car were waiting for them?

When they finally drew close enough to the building to see the parking lot and she didn't see either of the vehicles she had been dreading, Theresa felt a rush of relief. There *was* a car there that didn't belong, a newer crossover that she had never seen before.

Grace tensed beside her, even as she said, "It's normal for people to have guests over. It probably doesn't mean anything."

"Yeah," Theresa said, trying to convince herself. "We can't get worried every time we see a car we don't recognize, not when we live in an apartment building, for goodness' sake."

She and Grace exchanged a glance as they turned into the parking lot. She parked in her customary spot, and they got out of the car. Grace went around to the back to get Atticus out while Theresa walked around the crossover. It was a rental, which supported the idea that it was just someone who was visiting.

Grace looked nervous as she approached the front door, but Theresa didn't know if that was just due to being back at the apartment in general, or because of the strange car. Her friend jolted to a stop as soon as she pushed the door to the building open and Theresa had to look over her shoulder to see why.

Monica was waiting for them in the hall, and behind her, Grace's apartment door was wide open.

CHAPTER TEN

"What is she *doing* here?" Grace hissed.

Monica was already walking toward them down the hall. Theresa didn't know her, but she thought she looked worried.

"Grace, thank goodness. I tried calling you, but your phone wasn't getting service."

"I told you to leave me alone. I don't want to talk to you or dad or anyone until this is all figured out. You shouldn't be here, Monica."

"Well, I wanted to talk to you, so deal with it," Monica said. "I was hoping we could have a discussion, but then I saw—well, look." She turned and gestured back down the hall, toward Grace's apartment. Grace frowned and moved closer to her door, then froze. Theresa saw the open door, the broken doorframe, and a glimpse of a mess inside the apartment. It was a horrible sort of déjà vu.

"This can't be happening again," Grace breathed. With a shaking hand, she pushed the door the rest of the way open. Theresa looked past her into the living room. At least there wasn't a body on the floor this time, but the apartment was trashed in a similar way to how it had been before. "Why can't you just leave me alone, Monica? Why are you *doing* this?"

"It wasn't me," her sister said. "I swear. I was coming here to talk to you, but then I saw the door like this. I went inside, but only to look for you. I was worried about you."

"I'm calling the police," Grace said, handing Theresa Atticus's leash so she could reach into her purse for her phone. Theresa stood back with the dog, her eyes roaming over the room as Monica spoke.

"Don't, Grace. Or at least not yet. Can we please just *talk* first?"

"Even if you *didn't* do this, someone did," Grace said, gesturing. "And I'm guessing it was the same person who broke in a few days ago and killed my friend. Why on earth would I delay calling the police?"

"Because it won't take long to just hear me out."

"You're delusional if you think I care more about what you have to say than reporting the *second* break-in to my apartment in a *week*. I'm asking you to leave. But stay in town. I have a feeling the police are going to want to talk to you again after this."

"Please, Grace, it's important."

Grace ignored her, dialing the emergency number. For a second, Theresa thought Monica looked like she was going to leave, but she crossed her arms stubbornly. "Maybe we can talk after the police handle this," she said. "If they're going to question me anyway, I might as well wait around for them."

And she did. The two sisters stood in stony silence while they waited for the police to arrive. Theresa took Atticus to her apartment again, then stood out in the hall to wait with them. Fights between family members were always an awkward thing to be caught in the middle of, and the knowledge that Monica might have been involved with a murder just made it worse.

Monica stuck to her story when the police arrived. The same detective from before came to the scene, but with nobody injured, nothing visibly missing despite the mess, and no witnesses among any of the other tenants of the building, there wasn't much he could do besides escort Monica out of the building. Theresa could see them talking to each other through the propped-open door out to the parking lot. Monica seemed upset, but finally got into her car and drove away.

The detective came back and told Grace, "I asked her to give you some space. If she continues to bother you, please call the station so we can have it on record. If she makes any threats against you, we might be able to file for a restraining over."

He told Grace he was going to send extra patrols by the apartment for the next couple of days and suggested that she look into getting some security cameras and reinforcing the door, if their landlord would let her. Then he left them with a promise that he would keep working on the case.

"Do you want help cleaning?" Theresa offered once he was gone, looking around at the mess.

Grace shook her head slowly. "Not right now. Maybe later, but right now, I just want to be alone. I need to think about what I'm going to do next."

Grace came over to get her dog back, but Theresa didn't see her again that evening. She was a little afraid Grace was just going to pack up and leave, but after all of this, Theresa didn't think she could blame her if she did. It felt like letting whoever was behind all of this win, but it would be better to let a dangerous stalker push her out of town than for her to lose her life.

CHAPTER ELEVEN

Theresa woke up in the middle of the night to the sound of a woman screaming. She lay in her bed for a moment, her heart pounding, but only when the familiar, booming barks of her neighbor's dog started up did she realize it hadn't been a dream.

She threw the covers off herself and hurried through her apartment, turning the deadbolt and shoving the door open, not even stopping to make sure it shut all the way behind her as she ran into the hall. When she reached Grace's apartment door, she tried the doorknob, but the deadbolt was engaged. She started knocking on the door.

"Grace? Grace, are you alright?"

She was starting to wonder if she needed to give it up and call the police when she heard the deadbolt turn and Grace pulled the door open, her eyes wide and terrified.

"You should go," she whispered. "He told me to let you in, but you should go."

"Someone's in there?" Theresa wasn't sure her heart had ever been beating so fast. Adrenaline made her palms prickle. "If there's someone in there with you, I'm not leaving. Who is it?"

Grace hesitated, then pulled open the door. Theresa saw a tall man with dark hair standing by the patio door. She'd only seen him close enough to see his features once, but it was enough to recognize him as the mystery man with the tan car. Her blood felt like it turned to ice. She couldn't imagine a single good reason for him to be there.

He saw her looking at him and nodded to her, as if in greeting. "You're welcome to come in, Ms. Tremblay. I understand you're worried about your friend. I just want to talk."

Grace shook her head, but Theresa wasn't the sort of person who could leave her friend alone in the apartment with a strange man who had come to her patio door in the middle of the night, so she stepped inside. "Who are you?"

"My name is Cameron Reed," he said. She hadn't been expecting an actual introduction. "I'm a private investigator. Up until a couple of days ago, I was working for your sister." He said this last to Grace, who stared at him.

"Monica sent you?" Grace's face twisted. "I *told* her I didn't want to talk to her."

"I resigned from the job today, but she wanted me to pass a message on."

"In the middle of the night?" Theresa asked. It sounded like he was trying to reassure them, but none of this was reassuring.

"I had a crisis of conscience."

"I don't get it," Grace said. "What's going on? What do you want?"

"To show you these." He took his phone out of his pocket, tapped the screen, then handed it to Grace.

She hesitated, then cautiously stepped forward to take it. When she gasped, Theresa came up to her shoulder to see what she was looking at. They were photos of someone in Grace's apartment, taken through her patio window. The person in the apartment was dressed all in black, with a black hood over their face, and it was too far away to tell any details, but it was evident that they were the ones who had broken in and trashed the place.

"I don't understand. Are these from today?" Grace asked after she finished scrolling through them.

"Yes. She had asked me to watch you sporadically. I'm not at liberty to say why, but there was no set schedule. She didn't know I was watching the building at this time."

"I don't get where this is going."

He grimaced. "When I realized I was witnessing a break-in, I took these photos and then retreated to the parking lot so I could be ready to trail the perpetrator if they left. I was planning to call the police and keep an eye on them until they left. But then … I saw Monica's rental car in the lot." He met her gaze. "I believe your sister is the one who broke into your apartment earlier today."

Grace stared at him. "She was here at the same time as the break-in? Why didn't you *say* anything?"

"I should have." He looked ashamed. "I was conflicted, since she was the one who hired me. I confronted her about it earlier this evening, and she denied everything, but I decided I was no longer comfortable working for her. I didn't feel right leaving without letting you know personally what I saw."

"Did you tell the police?" Theresa asked sharply.

"I will in the morning, before I leave town. I'm going to swing by the station and show them these pictures."

Grace handed the phone back to him, looking shaken. "Thank you for telling me about this."

"Be careful. I don't think your sister is who she pretends to be."

Cameron left after that, going out the patio door so he could avoid notice if Monica was watching the parking lot. Grace looked more shaken than Theresa had seen her since the day of the murder, so she offered to sleep on her couch.

"I just have to go grab my phone and my keys and lock my place up first," Theresa said. She left her friend with her watchful dog and hurried back down the hall to her own apartment to grab her things. It was late, but she wasn't tired in the least. Not anymore.

"I can't believe she stood in the hall and lied to my face about what happened," Grace said when she got back. "It's terrifying. I don't know what to do."

"The police will handle it," Theresa said firmly. "I think we should go to the station ourselves in the morning, though. That guy claimed he was a private investigator, but he never showed us any ID, and the fact that he didn't go to the police right away makes me wonder if he really intends to at all."

Grace, who was sitting at the dining room table trying to calm herself with a cup of tea, frowned.

"What would the point of all of this be if he's lying about being a private investigator? But what he told us doesn't make sense either. Why would Monica hire a PI to follow me, then go and do something completely insane like break into my apartment twice?"

"Maybe it's another way to intimidate you?" Theresa guessed. "I don't know. I don't think we should just trust him, though. We should at least make sure he made the report like he said he would."

Grace nodded. "All right. We'll do that first thing in the morning, but... I'm going to think seriously about leaving town after that."

"If that's what you want, just let me know what you need, and I'll help you," Theresa promised.

She was getting too old to sleep on couches, and when she woke up in the early hours of the morning, her neck was sore. She squinted her eyes open, feeling a moment's disorientation at waking in the mirrored twin of her own apartment. Then she noticed the shape looming above her. She jolted fully awake, her heart rate ratcheting up before she realized it was just Grace. Atticus smashed his cold nose into her face as he sniffed at her, thrilled to discover she had slept over.

"Sorry," Grace said, stepping back a little so she

wasn't looming over her. "I didn't mean to startle you. I was just trying to wake you up."

"What time is it?" Theresa asked, sitting up.

"Just after seven," Grace said. Today was Theresa's original day off, and taking Saturday off had given her an extra day, not a trade. It still felt a little strange to sleep in past when the crêperie opened. She checked her phone to make sure there hadn't been any trouble with the opening routine, but neither of her employees had messaged her.

"My sister called," Grace said.

She wondered why the other woman hadn't led with that. Theresa dropped her phone on the couch cushion beside her and looked up at her friend. "Did you answer?"

Grace nodded. "She wants to meet." She paused. "I told her yes."

Theresa frowned. "That's a terrible idea."

"I know. But ... she said she's willing to drop the entire matter of the money. She just wants to talk to me. If that's true, if she's really willing to stop, I need to hear her out. I still want justice for what happened to Molly, but more than anything, I just want to stop being so scared all the time." She took a deep breath. "I'm going to meet with her. Do you think we could meet at the bookstore?"

Theresa still thought this was a terrible idea, but she had the feeling Grace was going to do it whether or not she helped. So, she blinked the sleep out of her eyes, tugged her fingers through her messy hair, and said, "I'll call Liam and ask. I'm sure he'll say yes. But we need to come up with some sort of plan for when this goes horribly wrong."

Liam did indeed say yes, and he wasn't even annoyed that her call had woken him up. He was worried, though. Just like her, he thought it was a bad idea but knew Grace would go through with it with or without their help.

Theresa listened as Grace called her sister back and arranged to meet at the bookstore at nine. She didn't mention anything about knowing Liam. She made the suggestion sound like she was choosing another public place at random. Once the arrangements were made, Theresa returned to her own apartment, took the fastest shower in the world, got dressed, and then met Grace in the parking lot. Grace had Atticus with her, and Theresa envied the dog's excitement for their early morning adventure.

"Do you mind if we drive together?" Grace said. "We can take my car this time, I feel bad that Atticus got yours all furry yesterday."

"It's okay," Theresa said as she followed Grace

over to her car. "I like having him around, fur and drool and all."

They loaded Atticus up into the back seat of Grace's car, which was set up with a blanket and some toys for him. Theresa got into the passenger seat and buckled herself in as Grace pulled out of the parking lot. Grace kept drumming her fingers on the steering wheel nervously, and as they drove into town, Theresa only became more and more convinced that this was the worst idea she had ever taken part in.

"So, we're going to meet your sister, who we have reason to believe broke into your apartment at least once, possibly twice, and may have committed a murder." Theresa sighed. "I don't see how this could possibly go well."

"I know. I know this is a terrible idea. But if she threatens me, maybe we can take it to the police? I just can't not do anything, Theresa. You don't understand what it's been like to live like this. I'm going insane. I just want this to be over."

Grace was at the end of her rope. Theresa understood that, even if she didn't know how to help her feel better. But something her friend had just said gave her the first inklings of a plan. If Monica threatened her, maybe they *could* go to the police with it. But they would need evidence.

"I have an idea," she said, pulling out her phone. "What if Liam sets his phone up to record, and hides it in the back room? It's a cluttered room, so if you meet her back there, she'll never notice the phone sitting under some papers or in a box of books. If we record the conversation and she says something incriminating, we can go to the police with the recording."

Grace looked over at her, the first glimmer of hope in her eyes. "That's a great idea. We can ask her about Cameron as well and see what she has to say about him. I wish I'd thought to record our conversation with him last night. Hurry, call Liam. Let him know what you're thinking so he can get it set up before she gets there."

Theresa unlocked her phone and hit the button to redial Liam's number. She brought her phone up to her ear and glanced up just in time to see a vehicle speeding toward them from an opposing intersection.

She didn't even have time to shout before it hit her side of the car and sent them skidding into the curb.

CHAPTER TWELVE

The car ran up on the curb and jolted to a stop against a tree. Theresa's airbag went off in her face before she even really knew what was happening. All she could think of was getting out of the car. She fought against the airbag, unclipped her seatbelt, and threw the door open, falling out onto the grass.

She stumbled to her feet and then realized Grace was still inside the car. She spun around, and the sight of Grace undoing her own seatbelt filled her with relief. Grace looked just as shocked as she was, but thankfully she didn't seem injured. She opened the driver's side door and stepped out of the car. Atticus, shaking and with his tail between his legs, jumped out of the car door after her, and Grace grabbed for his leash and missed.

"Atticus!" she called out after him. "Atticus, come back."

The dog ran into the closest person's yard and hid between two overgrown bushes. Grace started walking over to him. Theresa looked away when she heard a car door slam and realized she had forgotten all about the vehicle that had hit them in the shock of the accident.

It was a black truck. She would have recognized it even if she didn't recognize the man getting out of it. Brandon. Grace's ex-boyfriend had run them off the road.

"Grace!" she shouted.

Her friend turned around and spotted Brandon approaching her across the grass. She froze, then started to back away from him.

"Brandon? What happened?"

"Are you okay?" he asked, his steps quickening as he approached her. Theresa blinked. She'd been expecting anger, not him asking if they were all right. "I'm so sorry. I didn't see you. You just blew right through that intersection."

"No, we didn't," Grace said, though she sounded a little unsure. "We stopped, and you had a stop sign too. You're the one who hit us."

"You just came out of nowhere," Brandon said. He reached Grace and pulled her to him in a hug. Grace just stood there, and Theresa thought she must feel as befuddled as she did.

"Wait, let me go," Grace said, pushing away from him. "I don't understand."

"Are you hurt?" Brandon asked. "I don't think your car is going to start. I'll help you take it to the shop, and I'll drive you wherever you need to go while it's getting repaired."

"Hold on," Grace said, stepping toward the bushes. "This is all going too fast. Just … let me get Atticus." She turned back toward the dog. "Atticus, come here buddy. It's okay. I know this was frightening, wasn't it?"

Theresa realized she'd just been standing there, stunned, and started walking around the car. She gave Brandon a wide berth. He shot her a dark look but didn't say anything as she joined Grace in trying to lure Atticus out of the bushes.

"Grace, he'll come out on his own. Your friend can catch him. We should get going. You should go see a doctor, make sure you're all right. Get in the truck, we can call a tow truck for your car on the way."

"What? No," Grace said, shaking him off as he grabbed for her hand. "I'm not going. Not yet. I need to make sure Atticus is okay. And, oh my goodness, Liam and Monica—we were supposed to meet them. This is all messed up."

Theresa remembered that she had called Liam's number just before the collision. She wasn't sure if the call had connected, but if it had, he must be worried sick. She thought her phone was still somewhere in the car, so she turned and started walking back toward the vehicle. She realized, vaguely, that she was probably in shock, but all she could think about was getting to her phone and letting Liam know she was all right.

She opened the passenger side door and started looking for her phone. She found it on the floor, the screen cracked but still working. It showed her the call to Liam was still connected.

"Theresa, thank goodness," he said. "What happened? What was that noise?"

"We were in a car accident. We're okay, but—"

She broke off when Grace shouted. Turning, she saw that Brandon was trying to pull her toward the truck, and she was trying to yank her arm away from him. Atticus let out a loud bark and charged forward out of the bushes, which made Brandon drop Grace and back away.

"I have to go," she said to Liam. "Can you call the police?" She told him which intersection they were at, then hurried toward Grace and Brandon.

"What's going on?" she asked as she neared them. Atticus was still standing next to Grace, barking, and she finally grabbed his leash. The dog seemed uninjured, just shaken.

"He keeps trying to get me to go in the truck with him," Grace said. "I told him I need to take Atticus home."

"I'm trying to make sure you're okay," Brandon said. He ran a hand through his dark hair. "Don't you see that you can't be alone right now? When will you just admit that you need my help? We never should have split up in the first place. I just want to help you, Grace. If you had just listened to me in the first place, none of this would have happened. I would have protected you. Your apartment would never have been broken into. Your friend would still be alive."

Theresa frowned. Everything he was saying struck a chord wrong in her gut. Grace was busy looking over Atticus, making sure he was okay, and didn't seem to hear.

Theresa thought about the cookie jar and the fact that the only thing missing had been the cash. Whoever had taken it must have known it was there. She and Grace hadn't been walking Atticus for that long; whoever broke in wouldn't have had time to search every nook and cranny in the off chance they would find some cash.

Grace and Brandon had dated for a while, for long enough that he certainly would have known the little things about her like where she kept her cash.

And despite his protests, she was *sure* that he had hit their car on purpose. There had been no horn, no screeching tires, nothing but the big truck coming at them from the side like a cannon ball.

"Grace," she said, suddenly certain they needed to get out of here. "Come on, Grace. We should go."

Grace looked up at her. "Yeah, you're right. We should report the accident and get looked over. I should take Atticus to the vet, just to make sure. Maybe Brandon can drop us off there."

"No, I don't think that's a good idea," Theresa said.

"You're welcome to stay here if you don't like it," Brandon snapped. He moved forward, grabbed Grace's arm, and tried to pull her up. "Come on, let's—"

Atticus started barking at him again, and Brandon let go of her. Grace frowned and stood up, crossing her arms. "What are you doing? Get your hands off me."

"Grace, I'm trying to take care of you. I forgive you. We can get back together. I'm just trying to show you that you need me."

"Don't listen to him," Theresa muttered, moving closer to her friend.

"He can drop you off at the bookstore. Monica will be there soon. I don't trust her, and Liam shouldn't have to deal with her on his own."

"I don't think it was her," Theresa whispered. She glanced at Brandon, and Grace followed her gaze. "He's been doing all of this to threaten you."

"If he was trying to threaten me, don't you think he would be more ... threatening?" Grace asked. "He's offering his help."

"He's not trying to threaten you into giving him the money. He's trying to convince you that you need him. He's trying to scare you into getting back together with him."

Grace froze. She looked over at Brandon, who was frowning at them, and something in her expression shifted.

"Sorry, Brandon. I'm going to stay here with

Theresa. We'll call the police and let them handle things."

"You can't be serious. I just want to help."

Grace backed away from him. "I meant it when I said I don't want to get back together with you, Brandon. Please just leave me alone right now. If you want to wait for the police with us, you can do that."

"Are you kidding me?" Brandon asked. "How can you possibly think you don't need me, after everything that happened? You have people breaking into your apartment, stealing from you, attacking your friends. You need someone there to keep you safe. You wanted to get married one day, right? I'll get you a ring. We can get engaged. We can even set a date for as soon as you want."

Grace jerked back at that. "You're just trying to get my money. It's been you all along, hasn't it? All of this, even Molly, it was some sort of sick game to convince me that I needed you back in my life."

"You *do* need me in your life," Brandon said. "Breaking up was a mistake."

"You didn't think it was a mistake until after I got that money from my mother! How did you even find out about it? Were you stalking me? Did *you* hire that private investigator and tell him to lie about my sister? Oh my gosh, how far does it go?"

"Don't talk like that, Grace." He moved forward again, but Atticus started barking, pulling at the end of his leash. Brandon swore. "You know what, I'm done playing nice. If you want to deal with all of this on your own, fine. You'll regret it."

"Is that a threat?"

Brandon glowered at her. "Is that what you need? An actual threat? If you don't get back together with me, you are going to regret it even more than you already do."

Grace gasped. "It *was* you. You killed Molly." She swallowed, her eyes filling with tears. "Why? I don't understand why you had to kill her. You didn't have to *murder* someone."

He laughed. "You're the most stubborn woman I know. All of this is your fault. I tried to be reasonable. I called you, didn't I? I told you I wanted another chance. If I'd known your mother was going to leave you a fortune so soon, I'd have proposed to you months ago. That money should be half mine, at the very least." He moved closer again, this time ignoring Atticus's barking. "Give me the money, Grace, or you're going to regret it. Your sister said you got around a million. Give me half. That's enough for me to get out of the country and get set up somewhere else. Half a million dollars, and you'll never see me again. I won't hurt anyone else you care about. I won't ever contact you again."

"You're working with my sister?" Grace asked, sounding betrayed despite the fact that she and Theresa had both thought Monica was behind all of this up until a few minutes ago.

"No." He laughed derisively. "She didn't know we broke up. She called me to get information on you and let slip about the money. I don't know anything about a private investigator either, but I figured if your own sister was trying to get money from you, I'd better hurry to get back in your life. That way, if she looked like she was getting close to winning the money away from you, I could offer to take it off your hands. Keep it out of her grasp. You should have just given me a chance." He stepped closer. "I didn't mean to kill your friend. I didn't even know she was there. I was just planning on breaking in, messing the place up a bit so you would be frightened and call me for help. The door was unlocked, so I went right in. I didn't realize your friend was there until she came out of the other room and saw me. I'd already started throwing things around, and she started yelling at me to get out. I gave her a shove, and she fell and hit her head on a chair. I felt bad about it, but I figured it would be a surefire way to get you to ask me for help." He shot a glare at Theresa. "I didn't realize you'd become friends with your neighbor. I guess I should have gone after her next."

"I can't believe I ever dated you," Grace spat, disgusted. "Get away from me."

He ignored her and started to move closer. Atticus kept barking, but Brandon stopped just in front of him and said, "Hey, buddy. You remember me? We're friends, aren't we? You're a good boy."

The dog calmed down enough to start sniffing his hand, and soon he started wagging his tail. Brandon smirked. "You forget that I took Atticus on runs almost every day back when we were together. Come on. Get in the truck, *now.*"

He reached out and grabbed her. As soon as his fingers were around her wrist, Atticus started barking again. He jumped up and bit the hem of Brandon's sleeve. Brandon tried to yank his arm away, but when the fabric of his sleeve tore, the dog just readjusted, getting a better grip.

Grace grabbed her dog's leash and started trying to pull him back. Theresa stepped forward and helped her. As soon as they got Atticus off of Brandon, he got up and started running for his truck.

Theresa had almost forgotten she'd asked Liam to call the police, but as soon as the first cruiser came around the corner, she realized he had come through for her again. Brandon threw himself into the driver's seat of his truck, but it was too late. The police had him boxed in and there was nowhere for him to go.

EPILOGUE

"Are you sure about this?" Theresa asked. It was a little late to ask, since Grace's apartment had already been stripped of anything personal and her friend's car was stuffed full of luggage.

"I'm sure," Grace said. She bent down and hugged Atticus, scratching behind his ears before planting a kiss on top of his muzzle. "I'll be back, but I have too many bad memories here now. I want to travel a little bit. See the country, maybe even see another country. And I know Atticus will be in good hands here with you while I'm gone."

"I'll be happy for the company," Theresa said. "I'm going to miss you. You'll call, won't you?"

"Of course," Grace said. "I'll have to, to check up on Atticus. It's only for a couple of months. I'm looking forward to a chance to get away. I've never had a chance like this before. I'm going to spend a week or two visiting Monica too."

Theresa knew things were still complicated between the sisters. Grace had finally spoken to her sister the day after Brandon ran them off the road. Monica had admitted that she originally hired Cameron to follow her and try to figure out if there had been any foul play in their mother's death, or anything she could use to get her hands on some of the inheritance Grace had gotten.

But once she realized someone else was after Grace, someone willing to kill for the money, she had started to have a change of heart. She'd gone over the day Brandon broke in a second time to try to have a genuine conversation with Grace about what was going on and had almost met the same fate as Molly. When talking to the police, they discovered she must have gotten to Grace's apartment just moments after Brandon left through the patio door. After Cameron confronted her about seeing her car in the parking lot during the break-in, she'd been so desperate to talk to Grace that she'd even promised to drop the matter of the money if her sister would just *listen* to her.

So Grace was willing to give her a chance and try to repair a relationship that had never had much of a chance to grow in the first place. Theresa hoped it worked out for her.

Grace took a deep breath and handed Atticus's leash over to Theresa. The dog looked up at Theresa, his tail wagging. This wasn't forever—Grace would be back in a couple of months—but she knew how hard this was for the other woman.

"I'll take great care of him," she promised. "You know Liam will too—he loves Atticus."

"You know, most casually dating couples don't adopt a dog together," Grace commented. "Even if it's a temporary dog."

"Plenty of people have split custody of pets," Theresa said. "Hush." The arrangement was that Theresa would drop Atticus off with Liam on her way to work in the mornings, then she would pick him up in the afternoon when the crêperie was closed. That way Atticus, who wasn't used to being alone for long periods of time, would almost always be around one of them. "I'm pretty sure Atticus will enjoy the arrangement."

"I'm sure he will too. I'd feel a lot worse about going on this trip without him if I didn't know he had you."

"Don't feel bad at all. He'd be a lot more stressed flying around the country with you than he will be here with me. Take care of yourself, Grace. I hope you have an amazing time on your trip."

"Thank you for being such a good friend, Theresa," Grace said, hugging her one last time. "I'll let you know as soon as I get somewhere interesting."

Theresa and Atticus stood in front of the apartment building, watching as Grace got into her vehicle. She was going to miss her friend, but she had a four-legged companion to focus on now, along with the crêperie. She had also volunteered to find someone to sublet Grace's apartment while she was gone, which should be an adventure of its own.

She reached down and scratched Atticus behind his ears. She didn't want him to have to watch his owner drive away, so she waved at Grace one last time and then tugged on his leash.

"Come on, buddy. Let's go inside. I'll show you where all of your stuff is in my apartment. Grace brought a whole basket full of treats over for you."

His ears pricked up at the familiar word, and he trotted ahead of her a little, leading the way back inside and into her apartment. She had a dog now, even if just for a few months. And she couldn't have asked for a better one.

Made in the USA
Columbia, SC
15 August 2023